The Smeds and The Smoos

Written by Julia Donaldson   Illustrated by Axel Scheffler

Scholastic Press • New York

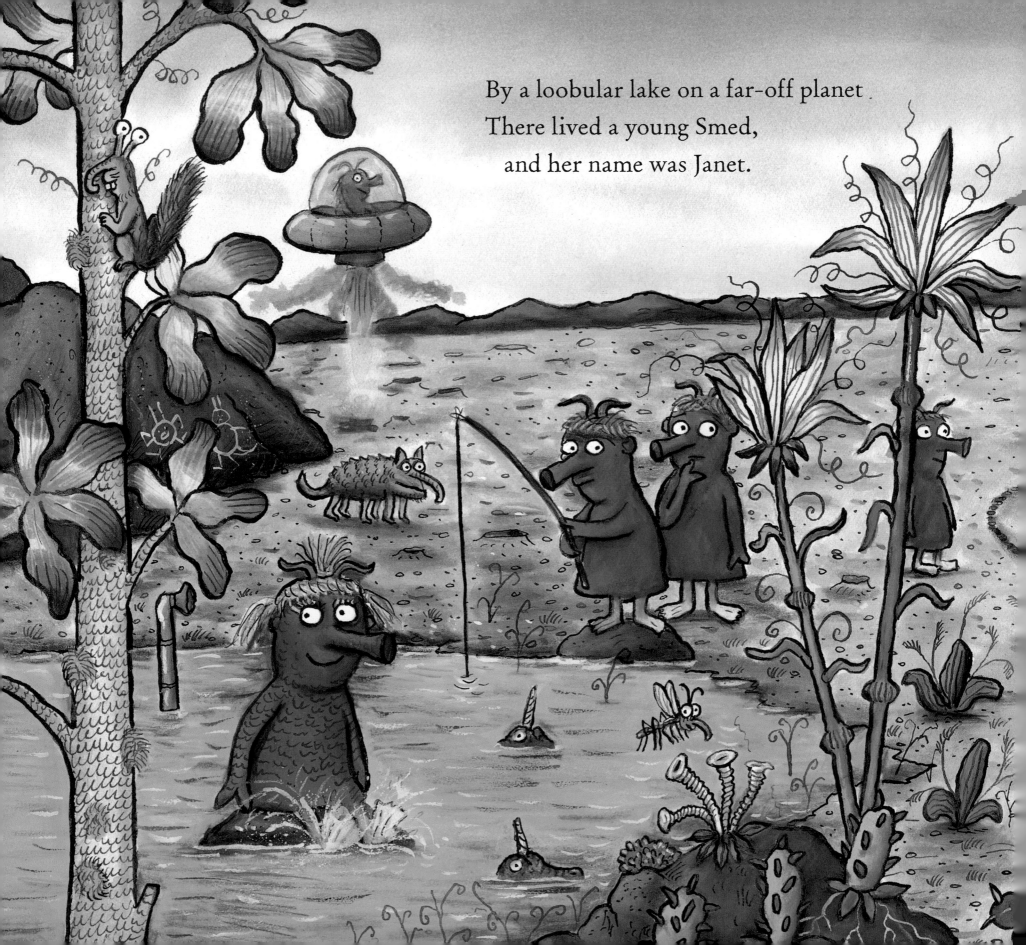

By a loobular lake on a far-off planet
There lived a young Smed,
and her name was Janet.

Not far away, on a humplety hill,
There lived a young Smoo
     by the name of Bill.

Janet, like all the Smeds, was red,
And this is what her grandfather said:

"Never, never play with the Smoos.
They sleep in holes. They wear strange shoes.
They jump about like kangaroos.
Never, never play with the Smoos."

Bill, like the other Smoos, was blue,
And these were the words
   of Grandmother Smoo:

"Never, never play with the Smeds.
They have strange hair upon their heads.
They sleep in funny things called beds.
Never, never play with the Smeds."

The Smeds on their lake liked nothing better
Than splashing about getting wetter and wetter.
But Janet grew bored with this watery play
And early one morning she tiptoed away.

The Smoos jumped about on their humplety hill.
They bounced up and down it and never stood still.
But Bill was beginning to think, "This is boring,"
So early one morning he set off exploring.

Janet met Bill in the Wurpular Wood,
Where the trockles grew tall
    and the glompoms smelled good.
The two rubbed antennae and played all day long.
She told him a story; he sang her a song.
Then they climbed to the top
    of a jerberrycoot
And nibbled its juicy
    and jellyful fruit . . .

. . . Till who should disturb them
but Grandfather Smed,
Shaking his fist as he angrily said:

"Never, never play with a Smoo.
They're such a nasty shade of blue.
For the hundredth time I say to you,
Never, never play with a Smoo."

Grandmother Smoo was close behind,
And this is how she spoke her mind:

"Never, never play with a Smed.
They're such a dreadful shade of red.
I'll say again what I've always said:
Never, never play with a Smed."

Years went by on the far-off planet.
Janet missed Bill, and Bill missed Janet.
But off they crept, whenever they could,
To sing and play in the Wurpular Wood.

The two of them grew
and decided to wed,
But what do you think
their grandparents said?

"Never, never marry a Smoo.
They're a beastly bunch!
    They're a crazy crew!
They drink black tea!
    They eat green stew!
Never, never marry a Smoo."

"Never, never marry a Smed.
My dearest child,
    are you off your head?
They drink pink milk!
    They eat brown bread!
Never, never marry a Smed."

Janet and Bill stole out that night
While their families slept
  and the squoon shone bright.
They clambered into the Smeds' red rocket.
(Grandfather Smed had forgotten to lock it.)
Bill pressed the button, and Janet steered . . .

. . . When their families woke, they had both disappeared!

The Smoos said, "Your Janet has stolen our Bill
And lured him away from the humplety hill."
The Smeds said, "It's Bill who has stolen our Janet
And taken her off to a distant planet."

The Smoos climbed into their rocket of blue,
And they said to the Smeds,
    "You had better come, too."

Suspicious and scowling, they soared into space . . .

. . . Till they reached Planet Vumjum, a dry, dusty place.

The Vums had long arms which they waved in the air,
But they didn't have news of the runaway pair.

The next stop was Lurglestrop, covered in roses,
And watered by beasts with small eyes and long noses.

They touched down on Grimbletosh,
coated in grime.

They searched Planet Glurch
and found nothing but slime.

One morning the Smoos found
they'd run out of tea,

So the Smeds shared their milk,
which was pink as could be.

Then Grandfather Smed said, "My hair needs a trim,"
And Grandmother Smoo kindly cut it for him.

They landed on Scloop,
   where the Scloopies wore kilts,

Then flew to Klaboo,
   where the Klabs walked on stilts.

They searched all year long,
   then they searched longer still,
But they didn't find Janet;
   they didn't find Bill.
"Alas," said the Smoos,
   and the Smeds said, "Alack!
We have failed in our quest.
   We had better turn back."

So they turned and flew home to their very own planet,
And far down below them, they saw . . .

. . . Bill and Janet!

The rocket touched down, and they ran to the wood
Where the trockles grew tall and the glompoms smelled good.
And there in a glade, by the rocket of red,
Were the runaway Smoo and the runaway Smed.
(They'd got lost and flown home again, only to find
That all of the others had left them behind.)

There was joy, jam, and jumping. Then Janet said, "Maybe
You'd like to make friends with our dear little baby?"
A baby! A red one? A blue one? But no —

That baby was purple, from head to toe!

They all hugged the Smoo-Smed,
  their new baby brother,
And Grandpa and Gran
  even hugged one another.
They laughed and they splashed
  and they danced with delight,
And they played with that baby
  from morning till night.
They made him a rattle. They made him a flute.
They fed him the fruit of the jerberrycoot.

Then they sang by the light of the silvery squoon,
And you can sing, too, if you make up a tune:
"Play with the Smeds and play with the Smoos.
Play with whichever friends you choose.
Then close your eyes and, while you snooze,
Dream of the Smeds and dream of the Smoos."

For the new Broughty
Ferry Donaldson
– J.D.

To all the children of
Europe
– A.S.

Library of Congress Cataloging-in-Publication Data available

ISBN 978-1-338-66976-3

10 9 8 7 6 5 4 3 2 1   20 21 22 23 24

Printed in Malaysia   108
First edition, November 2020

Book design by Zoë Tucker

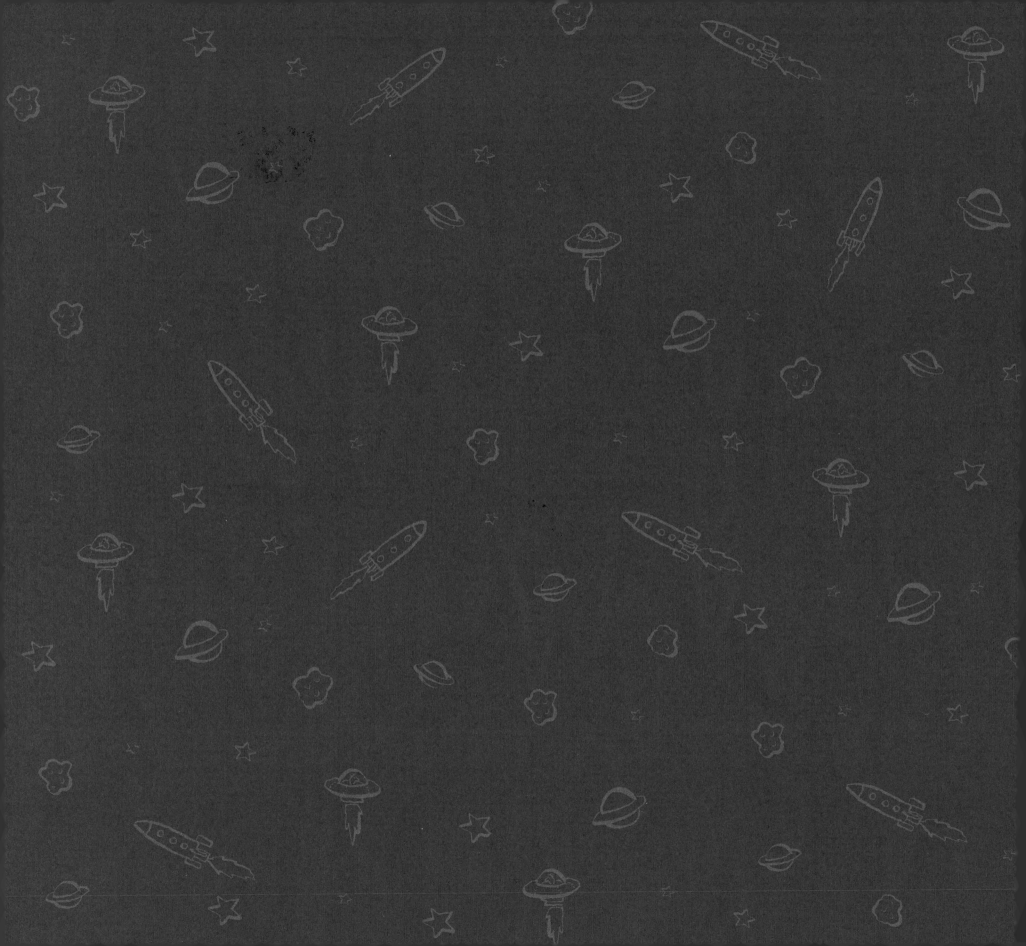